What About Me?

What About Me?

Gertie Evenhuis

Translated from the Dutch by Lance Salway

Illustrated by Ron Stenberg

THOMAS NELSON INC., PUBLISHERS
Nashville/New York

Copyright © 1970 by B. V. Uitgeversmaatschappij Deltos Elsevier

English Translation Copyright © 1974 by Longman Young Books

Text Illustrations Copyright © 1974 by Longman Young Books

Jacket Illustration Copyright © 1976 by Thomas Nelson Inc.

First U.S. edition

Library of Congress Cataloging in Publication Data

Evenhuis, Gertie.
  What about me?

  Translation of En waarom ik niet?
  SUMMARY: A young boy searches for a way to help the resistance movement in Amsterdam during the German occupation.
  [1. Netherlands—History—German occupation, 1940-1945—Fiction. 2. World War, 1939-1945—Netherlands—Fiction] I. Stenberg, Ron. II. Title.

PZ7.E914Wh4   [Fic]   76-27312
ISBN 0-8407-6524-X

Contents

1. My Brother and I...................................... 9
2. What About Me? 18
3. And Then, One Day 23
4. Dirk, Hero of the Resistance 29
5. The Next Morning 37
6. The Race Begins...................................... 45
7. Into the Country with Eddie 53
8. The Paper-Eating Pigs............................. 61
9. Roundup.. 72
10. The Child with the Star........................... 78
11. The Fight with Sebastian........................ 88
12. "I Wanted to Do Something, Too" 91

What About Me?

1

My Brother and I

It was the autumn of 1943 in Holland, and I was eleven years old. My name is Dirk.

My brother Sebastian was fifteen, and he had an identity card with his photo on it, and a fingerprint too. He was hard to get along with at the best of times, but now he'd become really unbearable. "You wouldn't understand these things," he'd say. "You're too young. We don't need you." He hardly paid any attention to me anyway, except to keep me out of his room. He thought he could do whatever he liked there. He had even sawn a trapdoor in the floor. And when I asked if it was supposed to be a hiding place for the British pilot who had escaped a short while before, he bit my head off.

We had all seen it happen with our own eyes: the airplane falling to earth like a flare, the white parachutes sailing alone through the sky. One of the pilots was caught by the Germans, and

they found another in a meadow just outside Amsterdam. All that was left of him, that is. The third one escaped. So my idea about the trapdoor wasn't so stupid, after all. But Sebastian lost his temper and kicked me out of his room, calling me a snooper and a busybody and telling me to get back to my kennel, and go and learn my multiplication tables. Multiplication tables! When you're in your twelfth year!

I knew perfectly well that my brother's friends came to his room in the evenings. I knew that they brought parcels with them and behaved very mysteriously. Sometimes Sebastian went out by himself. I knew for certain that he was delivering secret messages then.

Of course, I sneaked into his room when he was out. He had all sorts of things there—big maps of the Pacific Ocean, with Japan and Hawaii and so on. My uncle was a prisoner of the Japanese; he was my mother's brother and was so young that we just called him Hans.

Another map showed North Africa. The British and the Germans were there, each trying to push the other out. One of the German generals was called Rommel, a pretty stupid name for a general, if you ask me. We sang songs about him at school until Long John put a stop to it. He was our teacher. His daughter Johanna was in my class, too. She had green eyes. I liked her a lot, but I made sure that no one knew about it. I'd have died of shame if anyone found out.

Hawaii. When I saw names like that I longed to be on board a big ship. I'd be the captain. I'd force out the Japanese and free my Uncle Hans, who hadn't been heard of since he was captured.

My brother also had photographs of battle-ships; one of them was called *The Prince of Wales*. He had also made a model of a war fleet from paper and pins. I'd been allowed to help with that. And he had newspapers. They were dropped by planes at night and were called *Whirlwind* and *Flying Dutchman*. They were printed secretly in England. You weren't allowed to read them, and my father said that you could be sent to a concentration camp for less. They were thin, printed on cheap paper, and much smaller than ordinary newspapers. And they were just lying around in my brother's room!

He knew everything that was going on. He talked about desert troops and convoys, about Spitfires and U-boats. He also had a map of Russia, where the German armies had almost reached Moscow. My brother had pinned lots of little flags on the maps, and these marked the positions of the armies. Flags at Moscow, flags at Stalingrad. Flags in Egypt, flags in Spain and on Spitsbergen. The Germans seemed to be almost everywhere in the world.

He had to move the flags every now and then. The British would say that they had opened a new offensive and that the war was now just a matter of time. The Germans would say that everything was going according to plan and that Germany was winning on all fronts. And whether Sebastian was in a good mood or a bad temper would depend on the direction in which he had had to move the flags. They often moved in the wrong direction, and I was the one who suffered then.

This is what happened when I asked him for one of his secret newspapers. He had such a lot of them. Not that I didn't have anything of my own. After all, when we were staying with my aunt in the country, I had been the one who took the earphones from the cockpit of a crashed British bomber, just before the Germans descended on it like a lot of chickens. I was still a bit stunned by what I'd done. The earphones hung in my room. I had also taken a strange piece of glass that wasn't really glass and wasn't mica either. My mother wore it on a little cord around her neck, like a pendant. I was secretly very proud of that.

Well, anyway, I didn't get the newspaper I'd asked for. Such things were much too dangerous at my age, Sebastian had said, and anyway, I wouldn't understand half of it. I would let it lie around. I should just keep calm. I didn't need to know everything, after all.

This made me really angry. What was it that I shouldn't know about? They never told me. And what use was a brother who was four years older? Mend the tears in his black-out curtains—I was allowed to do *that*. Wear his old jackets. Run messages for him, I could do that too. Fight with him over our only bicycle, made from all sorts of spare parts. I had hoped that the bicycle could belong just to me, as I'd never had one of my own. Brother Sebastian had had the same idea. And what chance do you have against a brother who's so much stronger than you are? You always come off second-best.

Once, I used to look up to my brother. And I believed everything he said. But not anymore. He boasted a lot, too. Before the war, he used to say, you could eat as much chocolate as you wanted. You just threw bananas and apples away if you didn't feel like them. And there was no need to go to a farmer for extra milk or flour, no—the shopkeepers brought them to your door themselves! I could hardly remember what a banana looked like. There was white bread, Sebastian said, and there wasn't any clay soap or wooden combs. You could buy a complete suit and the shopkeeper would open the door for you with a bow. Toys? You just went into a shop.

Bread? You phoned the baker. The shops were crammed with things you could buy. Without ration books and without coupons. You didn't even need to stand in line.

I thought of the man who owned the candy store near us who, whenever he saw me coming, always shouted, "Everything's sold out! The shop's empty!" The last time, when my sweet ration was finished, I just bought some cough drops. I had stood in front of the shop window and said to myself, "I'll just have a pound of toffees. And ten bars of chocolate." Oh, well! I only had a ration card full of colored squares. And my mother looked after that. And a suit? My coat was fourth-hand, and my mother had turned my jacket until it was threadbare. She knitted new socks for me from my father's old underpants. And she had given up a sheet so that she could make me a white raincoat.

No, Sebastian needn't expect me to believe his stories. He said, for example, that the streets were brightly lighted at night before the war. And on holidays, such as New Year, the sky glowed with fireworks. Now you had to grope your way along hedges and walls, and read the house numbers with your fingers, as if they were written in Braille. Every now and again the searchlights from the defense artillery flashed above the pitch-dark houses. When the beams of light crossed each other they looked like a silver butterfly suspended there. Fireworks? Everything had been blotted out with thick black paper for as long as I could remember.

The grown-ups had this dream too. It always began with the words, *"Before the war . . ."* Just as our fairy stories began, "Once upon a time . . ." so their stories started with, *"Before the war, then* you could . . . *then* you were allowed. . . . *Then* you could buy what you wanted, stay out as late as you liked, say what you felt . . ."

Yes, perhaps. But it was wartime now and I couldn't believe that things had ever been different. That there had ever been nights when bombers did not drone over our heads and houses to Berlin and Cologne. And back again early in the morning. When there had been no thuds from the defense artillery and, now and then, airplanes screaming to the ground. When there had been no whispered conversations about strikes and secret printing presses and hidden radio transmitters. When there had not been at least one member of each family in jail for being "an enemy of the Reich." When people were not dragged from their houses on the slightest pretexts.

Now, German soldiers had it all their own way —in our streets, everywhere. Sometimes they took part in exercises outside the city, and I went to watch. The troops scattered over the fields, they set up their machine guns and shot at each other. They shouted loudly at the same time, with barking voices. Later, they stamped through the streets, their boots clumping on the stones. They sang, too, but—and this was so strange—even their singing sounded menacing and not at all cheerful. Even when the song was about a little flower. This is what they sang:

On the hillside grows a little flower (pom pom pom)
And it's called (pom pom pom)
E-ri-ca!

Their voices rose to a shout on the last syllables.

2

What About Me?

Anyway, I was seven years old when the war started. And I can remember quite clearly that there was shooting, and a lot of crying.

My Uncle Simon said that he had always known that the Germans would invade us, the swines, and that if he'd been in charge of the army it would never have happened. And my father said that we should never have surrendered.

My mother poured out cups of tea, added salt instead of sugar by mistake, and cried. "What chance did we have?" she said sadly. "Tanks, airplanes and soldiers, parachutists behind the firing lines . . . and all planned long beforehand."

"Well, what did you expect?" my uncle said scornfully. "We didn't have any proper defenses, did we? Just like the other countries that have been overrun. First there was Austria and Czechoslovakia, and then Poland. After that, Den-

18

mark, Norway, and Holland, Belgium a little while ago, part of France . . . They want the whole of Europe, that's what they want!"

My father didn't say very much, and he read the paper with a frown. He'd been a soldier himself and had seen a great deal. I hadn't seen anything much—just smoke, machine-gun fire, one bomb, blown-up bridges, burning houses. And two planes crashing over our street, one of them falling to earth in flames. Air-raid shelters. Smoke and broken glass. Searchlights sweeping across the sky. I had seen the German soldiers riding into Amsterdam on trucks and in cars. It was a splendid sight, the sort of thing you don't see very often. My brother stood behind me, watching them, and everything was different then. He used to tell me everything. And now?

"What about me? Let me do something too." So, at last, I had said it.

Sebastian, as unfriendly as ever, said, "What are you talking about now? *I* don't know what's going on. And you'd be better off knowing nothing at all."

But when you're in your twelfth year you're not stupid. I knew perfectly well that there was resistance to the Germans, that secret organizations had been set up to pass on secret papers, help pilots to escape, and look for hiding places for people who were hunted by the Germans. Otherwise they'd be sent to German prisons—just for one hostile gesture, one word spoken out of turn—or else they were taken to the German police headquarters in Amsterdam. Prisoners were tortured and murdered there, people said. I often thought about that at night when the planes droned over our heads.

Once I had seen for myself just how the Germans arrested people. If you could call it that. There had been a truckful of people in the street. Some of them were crying, but it was obvious that others were past caring. One man was trying to put on his jacket and it was fluttering behind him, but the Germans wouldn't let him stop to put it on. One soldier pushed the man from behind and kicked him. They hit him on the head with their clubs. Then they threw him into the truck because he couldn't climb into it quickly enough by himself. The people on the truck were Jews. I saw that the Germans were kicking them for no reason at all. I stood there as if I had been nailed to the ground. I hadn't realized that grown-ups kicked each other and threw each other into trucks.

When I got home, I was sick. And I started to have bad dreams at night. I didn't bother my parents with this, for they had enough on their minds already. My father's brother, Uncle Simon, had been arrested. He was dragged from his bed one night by the German police. No one knew why. My father took care to keep well clear of the Germans. He had been an officer in the army and he said that he didn't trust the Germans an inch, for all their sweet talk about being our protectors and wanting only the best for the Dutch. And my mother had to stand in lines for hours every day to buy things with our ration cards. And she had lots of other things to do as well.

So that's why I said to Sebastian one day, "Let me do something too." And I went on, "I really do know what's happening. I can write very neatly. I could do a marvelous chain letter. . . ."

My brother let out a great bellow of laughter. "You! A handwritten call to resistance! You've got to plan that sort of thing carefully. A network of . . . oh, what's the use of talking. We've got no use for children. Run along to school now."

He had said "we." *They* had no use for me. Yet, in my mind's eye, I could see myself writing the words: *Holland will not tolerate the depriva-*

tion of her liberty. . . . I muttered the words aloud. My brother heard me.

"I'm not a child!" I said. "I'm in my twelfth year, as if you didn't know. I know all about the man who wrote those words in that pamphlet. It's not everyone who'd be brave enough to say that."

"No," said my brother. "But he was executed soon afterward. Along with seventeen others. Now get off to school, I tell you."

3
And Then, One Day...

School! As if it were much fun there anymore!
The Germans had forbidden everything. We were
forbidden to have assemblies in the playground.
We were forbidden to sing the national anthem.
They tore out of the history books any pages
that mentioned the Queen or said anything
against the Germans. We weren't allowed to read
stories about some of our heroes of the past or
listen to music by Jewish composers. I had hardly
any friends, except for Eddie, and I didn't have
a dog either, for my mother said that it was
difficult enough to find food for ourselves.

That's how things were, and nothing much
happened at school—except for the time when a
boy was shot dead, quite by accident, in a crowd
of people who were trying to help some Jews to
escape. His name was read out at school; he was
called Ferry Verhagen and he was twelve years
old. The whole school had gone to the funeral,

the parents as well, and we all had to stand for hours because the Germans didn't trust us. They made the funeral cars leave very slowly at intervals of a quarter of an hour, and then they stood on guard all around the cemetery. The coffin was lowered into a deep hole. No one was allowed to say anything at the graveside. We mumbled the Lord's Prayer and that was just about all. It was late in the afternoon before it was over. And that was the only thing that had happened at our school. The teacher didn't have much time for us either, he probably had a lot of other things on his mind. No, nothing ever happened there.

So, when I heard one day that my brother's school had been taken over by the Germans, I was really furious. Why did everything happen to him, and nothing to me? He and two of his friends had been arrested two years before because they had worn white carnations on Prince Bernhard's birthday. They were held for hours, and beaten by the Germans, too. My father had been very angry, because it frightened him, and he asked Sebastian if he would mind displaying his royalist sympathies a little more discreetly in future. People ended up at the police headquarters for far less than that. Anything could happen.

And now his school . . . I cycled past it to see for myself and, sure enough, the whole school had been taken over, together with three houses nearby. There was barbed wire all around it and guard posts in front. German soldiers were on patrol. A deafening noise was coming from inside because a platoon was drilling on the marble floor. Boxes of eggs were being carried in through the main entrance. It really was so unfair that all the interesting things should happen to Sebastian.

"What were you doing near my school?" my brother said that evening. "I saw you there."

"Oh, marvelous!" I snapped. "I suppose that's forbidden, too?" And I chanted, "Staying out after eight o'clock—*verboten!* Listening to your own radio—*verboten!* Reading secret newspapers—*verboten!* Talking in the street to more than three people—*verboten!* And now riding past your school is *verboten* too." I pointed to the pile of newspapers and pamphlets on the windowsill. "But those things aren't *verboten* for *you,* it seems."

Sebastian looked at me coldly. "Forbidden to children, at any rate," he said for the umpteenth time.

"I know a lot more than you think I do," I

said, also for the umpteenth time. "Do you belong to a secret gang, Sebastian?" He didn't say no, and I went on breathlessly, ". . . that helps to hide pilots, that takes Jewish children to safety, that sends secret messages to England . . ."

He put his fingers to his lips. "Just remember one thing, Dirk," he said, and for once he didn't sound scornful. "The less you know, the less you can tell. Always remember that." He pointed to the newspapers. "I collect them. Sometimes we pass them on. It's the least one can do. . . ."

"Surely I can do a small thing like that, too . . . anything. You can trust me," I said, and I looked hungrily around his room for something to start with.

The bell rang.

"Do you have to get in my way all the time?" Sebastian said, suddenly on his guard. "I've told you, you can be arrested for much less than this. And if you give anything away, your whole family will suffer too. And now get out of here. You've wasted enough of my time already."

There was the sound of footsteps on the stairs.

"You're a pig, that's what you are!" I shouted, and slammed his door behind me.

Seething with rage, I ran into the street and

around the corner. "I won't stand any more of this!" I shouted to myself. I almost collided with two people. And you can believe this or not, but one of them dropped a piece of paper. He turned around to pick it up, but I was quicker. The man gave me a swift look. Then he shrugged and walked on.

I had the message. I unfolded the piece of paper nervously in a doorway. It was a call to strike but, in my excitement, I didn't notice what the reason was. But I did notice the heading in thick black letters:

> Comrades, pass this on when you have read it.
> Display it wherever you can.
> Do it carefully.

And then I knew what I had to do.

I waited until Sebastian went out that same evening. I crept into his room. If anyone should come in unexpectedly, I would say that I was only adjusting the black-out curtains. After all, there were posters everywhere that read:

This is Black-Out Week. Warn your neighbor if he is breaking the black-out regulations. If necessary, explain to him the dangers that can result. If you receive a warning because of your own carelessness, be grateful and do not say, "Mind your own business!"

A bulletin that was tailor-made for this moment, I thought gratefully.

I looked around hurriedly. Yes, there were the forbidden newspapers. I snatched a handful. It was the least I could do. After all, the pamphlet had said, "Pass this on." I would be able to do something for my country at last. I might not be able to kill Hitler, but I could do something to help. They said that you could wish someone's death by thinking evil about them. Or by piercing their photograph with a pin at midnight by a full moon. But I didn't have a photograph of Hitler. My father said that he wouldn't allow such things in his house. Never mind. I could do something much better now. I would show them all that someone in his twelfth year isn't a child anymore.

With seven papers and a tube of glue I crept out of Sebastian's room. I had the exciting feeling that I had now become a member of the Resistance, someone who casually risked his life for his country.

4

Dirk, Hero
of the Resistance

I gave the first paper to Long John at school
the next day. He gave me a searching look with
his gray-green eyes, but he didn't say a word.
He pushed the paper into his pocket.

The teacher's name was De Lange, but we
called him Long John, because he was tall and
thin. He had black hair and a big hooked nose.
His eyes pierced right through you. Whenever he
looked from left to right, his gaze moved just
like a searchlight. He saw everything. His voice
wasn't loud, and he didn't laugh very often. If
we had been younger, we would have been scared
to death of this serious dark man with the thin
face. But we had gone through a lot with him
and we knew that there was laughter behind
those bushy eyebrows, and that when he was
really amused he just drew up one corner of his
mouth.

When he had pushed my newspaper into his

pocket, he said to the class, "Page seventy. And before I forget, tear that last dictation out of your exercise books. No-o-o-o, you fools. Not the whole book, they don't grow on trees, you know. And don't leave a margin in future. The new exercise books seem to be made of toilet paper, so we want to make the most of those you've got. So, just the last dictation."

I looked at it. It read, "Holland will rise again, and our Queen will soon return to us by airplane from England."

"Is the inspector coming, sir?" Johanna asked, as she tore out the page. She usually called her father "sir."

"I don't know," Long John said vaguely. "But it's better to be safe than sorry, don't you think? Now, page seventy."

He looked around the class with an expressionless gaze. He was very hard to understand. Some people said that he took part in the Resistance, that he went about after dark in search of places for people to hide in, people who were hunted by the Germans. They said that he helped to forge identity cards, and stole ration books, and that he sent messages by courier to secret addresses, to the leaders of the Resistance. I didn't know whether any of this was true or not.

The only thing I had ever heard him say about these things was, "Now listen, good is good and evil is evil. And national socialism is worse than evil."

"He'd better watch his step," Gerard Drongers had said when he heard this. Gerard was the only Nazi boy in our class. "They broke up a whole gang of people like him not so long ago."

I was glad that Long John had one of my papers in his pocket.

When it was dark I set out with the other six. Distribute them as quickly as possible. Pass them on. The British radio had said this too. So I pushed a paper into the first letter box I came to in my street. But as soon as I had done it, I clapped my hand over my mouth. How stupid could I get! That wasn't a very clever beginning for a hero of the Resistance. A traitor might be living in that house. No, I had to distribute the remaining papers with a bit more sense. I would give one to the milkman on the corner near us. He always fell over backward to be as fair as possible to everyone. "Black market? Over my dead body," he always said. And he always did everything that the Queen told us when she broadcast from England. I gave him two papers;

he'd be sure to pass one on. I wrote "One extra"
on one of them just to make sure.

Now one for Amanda, the girl in my class who'd
been evacuated from Rotterdam after the bomb-
ing. She lived with her uncle and aunt, and already painted her nails. Her mother had been
killed by a bomb. Her little brother was always
playing parachutes with an old umbrella, and he
liked to pretend that he was a German coming
down over the city. He was hardly six years old
and didn't really understand much, but Amanda
always got angry with him just the same. "Can't
you do something else?" she'd shout. They had
gas masks as well, those two. I'd never seen such
things before. Their father had escaped to England in a small boat. Both children always became hysterical whenever they heard an airplane.

"I wish I could have gone to England in a boat,
too," I'd said to Eddie once. But he said that
it wouldn't have been much fun, really, zigzagging
through minefields, and torpedoes, and German
warships, and not being allowed on deck. "And
besides," he had added reproachfully, "you can't
even swim!"

Now I had two left. It was all going very well
indeed. Who next? Johanna? No, that was a stupid idea. Her father had one already. It wouldn't

do to waste my valuable supply. Wait, what about Bongers, the fruit-and-vegetable man? He often gave me an extra apple. I ran to his street. Just one sheet left now.

A big billboard loomed up out of the darkness in front of me. What had it said in the pamphlet? *Do it carefully.* I felt in my pocket. The tube of glue was still there. I smeared some on the paper, keeping it hidden under my jacket. I stood

and waited. The billboard was covered with posters, which I pretended to read. There wasn't a
single space left. Well, it would have to go on
top of a picture of Hitler. There was no one near.
I whisked the paper from under my jacket and
stuck it onto the billboard. I smoothed it quickly
with my hands. It didn't look very neat but at
least it was there. Hitler had been a paperhanger,
too. Or had he been a painter? Now who had
told me that? I took a last look at my handiwork
and then crept quickly away to our street.

I soon came in sight of the chink in our black-
out curtains. But there was a black shape moving
in the doorway. Who could it be? I had to pass
it to go inside. Someone was probably checking
on the number of the house before ringing the
bell. No, the figure was moving away. It was
coming toward me. I turned around and started
to run. Then someone grabbed me by the collar.
Before I could scream, I heard his voice. It was
Meertens the milkman.

"Hey, you!" he said. "You really ought to keep
your door shut! I had to bring your mother some
more cheese and your door was standing wide
open. I'm always warning people to keep their
doors closed day and night. Anything left behind
an open door can be stolen in a moment. Coats

from the hooks, shoes . . . I always carry my milk can all the way up the stairs, otherwise it'd be gone before I could turn around. And your door was wide open! What are you doing out at this hour, anyway?"

"The mail . . . a letter . . ." I mumbled, and slipped inside. My heart was hammering. For a moment I had thought he was suspicious. I would have to be much more careful in future. But this was only the beginning, after all.

I went to bed content. The droning of the British planes sounded like music in my ears. All night I dreamed of armies that marched over the sea, of heroes and soldiers, and of the Dutch people passing papers on to one another.

I was still elated when I arrived at school the next morning. I was so excited that I didn't think it odd to find the whole class crowded together in a corner of the playground.

"Assemblies *verboten*!" I called out recklessly.

Someone turned around. "The teacher's been arrested. He's at police headquarters. He had forbidden papers."

Who had said that? Aart, Eddie, or Amanda? I felt as though I had been hit on the head with a hammer. The blood seemed to drain from my body. I held fast to the school gate.

"What's wrong with you?" Amanda shouted in fright. "Hey, look at him . . . he's gone so white, like a piece of chalk . . ." She came toward me.

"Er . . . nothing . . ." I stammered. "Been running too hard, I expect." I turned around and pretended to look for my handkerchief.

Amanda shrugged her shoulders and wandered away. I pressed my hand to my heart. It was thumping, thumping like mad, as if it were trying to burst from my body. The teacher. The teacher had got those forbidden papers from me. From my brother. From the Resistance. From . . . I shut my eyes tightly.

5

The Next Morning...

It had never been so awful at school before, even though we had free periods all morning. My mind raced with images. I saw the teacher in a striped convict suit. His head was shaved bare. Then I saw myself . . my brother Sebastian being deported on a train . . . the hand of the German who came to arrest me. I could feel his breath on my neck.

As if from a great distance I could hear the others talking. The shrill voice of Wanda de Wit rose above the rest: "I heard all about it, didn't I? In a patrol car . . . dragged out of bed . . . police headquarters . . ."

The teacher had given me such a strange look when he folded up the paper.

". . . he'd been collecting money for pilots. . . . No, no, for Jews. . . . Wasn't it for people in hiding? . . . There were two of them in his house. . . . Look, you don't know what you're talking about. . . ."

"Did you hear about that pilot who escaped disguised as a monk?"

"They're taken away in cattle trucks . . . in a boarded-up train. . . . If you're in the crowd you can throw them bundles of clothes. . . . That train . . . where does the train go then? The train that never stops, the death train. . . ."

I saw it now in front of me, as clearly as if I were really standing there. Who had told me about it? I saw a room where the furniture had been turned upside down. Bewildered children were sitting on piles of belongings, a mother had two children on her lap, one of them was crying. A small group of people shuffled toward the train. There were Germans in front and behind, armed with clubs and guns. The Germans were much bigger than the people. A small child hung on to her mother's hand and from her hand a doll, a rag doll, hung in its turn. . . . Where did these pictures come from? Who had told me about it all? The bare heads of the prisoners, the black shadows of the Germans . . .

"No, no, those were Jews," someone said loudly. "What do they really do to them, anyway?"

"Well, they keep them prisoner for a while,"

said Jaap Hansen. He knew because his uncle had escaped from one of those camps. "And then they gas them, don't they? Or kill them some other way. Well, gas is the quickest. My uncle told me all about it. He said that they have shower rooms there. Except that gas comes out instead of water. Sometimes . . . you don't believe it, do you? But you can see the smoke from the chimneys. And my uncle says you can smell *human* . . ."

"Hey, can't you talk about something else?" Ina van Dam shouted suddenly. "Can't you see that Johanna . . . Johanna . . ." She sank back in her desk. "Johanna isn't here," she said softly.

"No, but *we're* here," Amanda said. "You and your creepy stories. . . ."

"They're not stories," Jaap said calmly. "They've got other ways of doing it. You draw lots, to go right or left. If you go left you're shot dead, if you go right you have to work on the land. Then you're lucky, of course."

"Depends what you mean by lucky," someone interrupted. And Jaap had to agree.

Ina started to cry. "It's a shame," she sobbed. She stamped her foot on the wooden floor. "And you!" She turned on Gerard Drongers. "What are *you* doing here, anyway?"

"You want to know something?" Gerard said. "Those Jews, they're all swindlers. Those things don't happen to Aryans. My father says . . ." Ever since his father had joined the Dutch Nazi party, Gerard felt brave enough to say anything he liked. Every Saturday he stood on a street corner and sold copies of the Nazi newspaper *Nation and Fatherland.*

"You should be ashamed of yourself!" Wanda de Wit shouted with a catch in her voice. "I saw you on Saturday, in your Nazi monkey suit. With your hand held high for the Führer. You . . . you should be ashamed. You're turning against your own people."

Gerard laughed mockingly. "Oh, yes? And what are *you* doing for your country? Walking around with carnations on the Prince's birthday. He's done nothing for his people. Wearing orange bows in honor of a Queen who's run away. Wilhelmina isn't coming back! And my father . . ."

"Oh, leave your father out of this," someone shouted.

Wanda began to sing mockingly:

> "On the corner
> of the street
> stands a Nazi.
> It isn't a man

It isn't a woman
But it's nasty.
He's selling papers
to ladies and gents.
Selling his 'fatherland'
for six red cents."

Gerard really lost his temper now. He rushed out of his desk and screamed, "Don't you know who you're talking to? My father could have all of you arrested!"

Suddenly all the fear and tension of the morning welled up in us all. Shouting and swearing, we rushed at Gerard Drongers, who instantly disappeared beneath us. We were all screaming and crying without knowing exactly why. It may have been from despair or from anxiety about our teacher. And if the teacher from the next room hadn't come in at that moment, who knows what might have happened. Anyway, the teacher gave us work to do and kept his eye on both classrooms. He didn't say a word, but his brow was furrowed, and when he tried to write on the blackboard his chalk broke. We all sat miserably at our desks.

I don't really know how I got through that morning . . . that morning at school. . . . I expected them to come for me at any moment. I froze at each sound, at each footstep in the street. "Your teacher gave us your name . . . your brother . . . your father . . . and your mother are . . ." Poor Long John. Who could blame him if he talked? Could I hold my tongue if they pulled out my nails one by one? Or stubbed out their cigarettes on my arm? The teacher . . . they would beat him, he would have to endure the most terrible things. . . .

I shivered, even though I was sitting next to the stove. The teacher looked at me curiously. "You can eat your sandwiches now, if you like." But I shook my head. I couldn't think about food. Would they send me parcels in the camp? Black bread, and bacon? No. What was the use of food when you were going to be shot the next morning? I looked around the classroom. Would they miss me? Would the teacher read out my name, as he had done with Ferry Verhagen? *Boys and girls, I have to tell you that your classmate Dirk Waterman* . . . No. It didn't sound the same.

Noises again. A car stopped outside. I jumped up. And I wasn't at all surprised when the lady who taught the fourth grade came in and whispered to the teacher, "There's a patrol car outside again. . . ."

Resigned to my fate, I sank back in my desk. If it had to happen, then let it be as quickly as possible. Were those footsteps in the passage? But the patrol car was still waiting outside an hour later.

". . . the teacher gave us your name . . . he's been beaten up . . . your brother has already been deported . . . the house has been searched . . . the earphones have been found and also . . ."

There was a sudden sharp noise. Someone blew a whistle. A platoon of soldiers came rumbling into the street. I felt very calm now. So they were there at last. The song came nearer and nearer, I felt myself being caught up in it:

> "When the soldiers
> march through the town . . ."

They marched nearer, stamping and singing. Soon they would come to a halt, barked words of command would ring out, heels would be clicked together. They would surround the school, shout *Heil Hitler!* and stamp up the steps, into the classroom, with green helmets. One of them would beckon to the teacher, shout, *"Wo ist Dirk?"*

But they marched right past.

"They . . . they're not stopping," I whispered to Eddie.

He looked at me. "What's wrong with you? Don't they go to the swimming pool every Thursday?"

I wiped the perspiration from my forehead. Yes, of course. Every Thursday.

I ran home as fast as I could. My legs felt as though they would give way at any moment. I hoped against hope that there was still something left to save. Perhaps the house hadn't been searched after all. Perhaps my brother had only been sent to a labor camp. . . . Not that that would be much fun! I hadn't realized before how much I really loved my brother. And then I became suddenly calm. I knew exactly what I had to do. Every suspicious piece of paper, every forbidden pamphlet had to come out of his room. Every newspaper. Every manifesto. If he wasn't at home, that is. *If my brother wasn't at home . . .*

I crept up the stairs.

6

The Race Begins

I was in luck. Sebastian wasn't at home and my
mother told me that he would be out for the
entire afternoon. That was even better. It was
almost as if Sebastian himself were offering me
his things with a polite bow. I knew that he would
be furious, but that didn't worry me anymore.
It seemed very unimportant when I thought of
the deadly danger that threatened him without
his knowledge.

I went through his room like a tornado. I
grabbed papers from his table and from his closet,
and I even peered into the hiding place he had
sawn in the floor. Perhaps there really was a pilot.
. . . I struck a match and shone it inside, holding
my breath. A mouse scampered busily away.
There was nothing else there apart from some
empty cartridge cases.

I collected all the papers together and stuffed
them into my pockets. They rustled as I went

downstairs. A small fire was burning in the
kitchen stove; I opened the door and pushed two
newspapers inside. The fire consumed them noisily, and then I heard voices and stopped to listen.
The walls of the kitchen were very thin. My Aunt
Tina had come to see us. I waited, listening carefully.

My father was telling her about something he'd
seen in the street. He sounded very excited.

"The swines," I heard him say. "Another
roundup of Jews."

"Just one of many," my mother said softly.
"It happens day and night . . ."

"Yes," said my father. "And it won't be the
last."

I could see him now—his thin, slightly stooping
body, his bowed head, his mouth a thin line. He
always took everything very much to heart.

". . . I was so angry, so angry inside, but I
couldn't do anything, I didn't even shake my fist.
I was beside myself. And yet I did nothing. . . .
It's shocking to live at a time like this, when
people are turned out of their homes like dogs.
With trunks and bags. Children with their
dolls . . ."

"Near us," said my aunt, "near us, a man and
a woman were taken away. The children were
left behind. If *I'd* been there, I would . . ."

"And no one put out a hand," my father repeated. "People just went on with their shopping. I saw it myself. And I? That's the worst part." I could hardly hear him now. "I wanted to be shot by the Germans too. Along with the Jewish men . . ."

"No," said my Aunt Tina. "No, Aart. What would have happened to Ella and the children then? But I know how you feel. I haven't any children. Yet if ever I saw something like that again, children who've been left behind all alone . . . you have to be careful, but even so . . ."

"What on earth is that smell?" said my mother.

I panicked. I had a half-blackened newspaper in my hand when my mother came into the kitchen.

"Oh, no, Dirk, not in there," she said. "It's hard enough to keep the stove going at all without you putting rubbish in it as well. . . ."

I prayed that she wouldn't want to take a closer look at the "rubbish." My prayer was answered—she took the teapot, filled it with ersatz tea, patted me on the cheek, and disappeared into the passage.

"That didn't get me very far," I muttered to my bulging pockets. "I'll go to Eddie's. I'll see what I can get rid of there."

But halfway down the hall I remembered

something and ran upstairs again, to my room this time. The earphones! Those would have to go too, and quickly. What if the Germans spotted that they'd come from a British plane? Everyone knew how anxious they were to find escaped pilots. They'd obviously think that I'd had contact with one of them. Especially if they found the trapdoor in Sebastian's room as well. No, the earphones would have to go into the canal. I pushed them into my inside pocket. It would be a terrible sacrifice. But there was nothing else to do. And I shouldn't be so soft-hearted anyway. I should be grateful that I was still alive.

I had to wait by the drawbridge over the canal for a ship to pass by. Gigantic letters painted across the bridge read: *GERMANY IS WINNING ON ALL FRONTS!*

"Pigs!" I muttered. "And now they want my earphones too."

And then, suddenly, they slipped from my hands into the water. "Damn!" I said out loud. I almost started to cry. I bit my lips.

"What did you say?" asked a voice behind me. Startled, I turned around. It was Meertens the milkman.

"Someone fallen in?" he asked with interest. It was amazing how curious he was about everything.

"Hmmmm," I mumbled. It now came home to me that my British earphones were gone forever. I looked sulkily at the bubbles that had risen to the surface of the canal.

"I don't suppose it was a German?" the milkman asked. I laughed, in spite of myself. Then I grew angry again. "No. It's my earphones. They came from a British plane."

"What on earth made you come here with something like that? It's a crying shame that they should be lying down there." Together we peered into the water. "If you want to know, I pulled a German out of there not so long ago," he said.

I looked at him in anger. A German? Someone who frightened people? Who prohibited everything? Who stole our clothes, our food? Who collected cartloads of Jews as if they were refuse? And *he* pulled one out of the canal?

"I heard a friend of mine shouting that one of 'em had fallen in. 'Let him drown,' I said. Yes, just what you're thinking now. Yes, boy, I know they're to blame for everything. But, well, there are limits, after all. Perhaps he'd been drowning his sorrows. I've seen it before with boys in the army, dead drunk and falling in the canal because they couldn't walk straight anymore. So I ran up here. And his head was still above water, over there by that bank. So I went and hung over the railings and stuck out my arm. Can't reach you, I shouted. It was pitch dark too. So I climbed over and hung from the railings with my legs dangling in the water. I was nearer then. The fellow grabbed me by the trousers. And what d'you think happened? Would you believe it, he pulled my trousers off. Yes, he did. Well, what could I do? It was still pitch dark, so I thought, what does it matter?—no one could see anything anyway. And I hauled him out. Pleased he was, too. Wanted me to go back to the barracks, have a drink with him and all that. No, mate, I said. *Was?* he shouted in amazement. I don't want anything, I said. I'd do the same for a dog. But he wrote down his name for me, and his unit. I put the bit of paper in my pocket and off I went. I didn't trust the fellow farther than I could see him."

He fumbled in his pockets and pulled out a crumpled piece of paper. The note from the German soldier. This reminded me of the contents of my own pockets.

"I—er—I've got to go," I said.

"Yes, but let me tell you . . ."

"No, no, I've got to go, it's urgent," I shouted over my shoulder. I left the milkman disappointed behind me.

I ran so hard that I got stitches in my side. So I stopped for a while in a shop doorway. I read the notice that hung there. I always read everything I saw, even scraps of newspaper in the street.

Anyone who manufactures or distributes writings, pictures, or other items that are hostile to the Third Reich, or has such items in his possession, will be punished with imprisonment. . . .

I didn't read any further. Perhaps someone had already found out about me. I had to hurry. Now. The Germans might be searching for me at this moment. I rushed on. The prison loomed up on my right. There was a church opposite. If only I could have disappeared inside! But I ran on. I had to get to Eddie's house.

7

Into the Country with Eddie

Eddie was my friend. He was a dreamer, he lived in a world of his own. He wrote poems and was always full of bright ideas. Nothing ever came of them, and the next time we met he would have thought of something else. His father was a prisoner, and so Eddie was the apple of his mother's eye. Whenever he had to go and buy milk from the farmer, she showered him with instructions and warnings. And this was what was happening now.

While they skirmished in the hall, I pulled a newspaper from my pocket and shoved it into their kitchen stove. The stove began to roar like thunder. I pulled out a second paper. And then Eddie drawled: "Come on, let's go. What are you doing with the stove, anyway? It's smoky enough in here as it is."

I pretended to be warming my hands. Eddie's mother called out that he should put the milk

bottles in the saddlebag and cover them with old
rags. Eddie shouted back: "Yes, Ma."

She came into the kitchen. "Oh, there's Dirk.
You're not cold, are you? Well, it *is* chilly for
this time of year. Here, lad, have a mug of hot
tea."

I took a few steps back and gulped my tea
noisily. There was a sudden noise in the passage.
Eddie's brother, Karel, was shouting, "Look what
that blasted brother of mine has done now!"

"Oh, what's going on now?" said Eddie's
mother. "Always calling each other names. Fred
van Dis's mother told me only yesterday that
Dirk and his brother get on so well together. So
why do you two have to fight all the time? Switch
that radio off, Karel. Come on, Eduard, off you
go now."

I was very nervous. I edged backward toward
the door.

". . . and make sure nothing gets stolen. I've
heard that they even take milk away from children. Dronger's eldest boy has joined the Nazi
Home Guard now. He should be ashamed of himself. He's twenty-one and can do what he likes,
he says. And he's so rude to his father. But then
he's so stupid anyway. Helping the Germans.
Taking milk from children! As if we don't get

little enough as it is. Look, I was reading in the paper about what you can get for your coupons. . . ." And she began to read out a long piece about barley and beans and groats. "Oh, are you leaving now, Eduard? Give my regards to the farmer. And put on your sweater, it's cold."

And so off we went. The tea sloshed around inside me. Eddie was riding his old child's bike with enormous tires, and I collected my father's bike as we went past my house. I couldn't reach the pedals properly, so I had to ride hanging between them and the saddle. The houses glided by, and sea gulls skimmed over the roofs.

When we reached the prison, Eddie turned around and said, "Who'd want to be in there now, hey? Behind those barred windows . . . When d'you think they'll . . ."

"Dunno. When the war's over. My father says it can't go on much longer."

"Yes, but that's what they said about the Spanish. And they stayed in the Netherlands for eighty years."

The papers rustled as I pedaled. I looked at the houses again. Just suppose I were to ring one of the doorbells. "Excuse me, can I leave some papers with you?" "Who are you, then?" "I'm a friend of your son's." "Oh, all right, just put them down there." No, it couldn't possibly be as easy as that. But Eddie's talk about the Eighty Years' War had given me an idea. Didn't the Dutch rebels eat messages to stop them from falling into the wrong hands? I wanted to ask Eddie about this, since he knew a lot about history, but I couldn't. The less he knew the better. Carefully, I pulled a paper from my pocket, crumpled it tightly and put it into my mouth. With renewed confidence, I started to chew.

Eddie began to let off steam about his brother's arrogance. And then he had a new idea—we should form a secret gang to free Long John from prison. After all, we were the ones who knew him best. He looked at me expectantly.

"Hmmmm," I said with my mouth full.

Eddie stared at me in amazement. "Hey, what have you got there? You're not *eating,* are you?"

His eyes bulged with indignation. I burrowed in my pocket. By a stroke of luck I found a few wheat kernels underneath the papers. At that time we used them instead of chewing gum. If you chewed them for long enough they became quite soft. Satisfied, Eddie took some kernels from my outstretched palm and put them in his mouth. I chewed like a mad thing. It was going to be harder than I expected to eat up all those newspapers. It was just as well I'd had that tea. They'd mix well together.

"Perhaps he was secretly in touch with England," said Eddie mournfully. "There were some boys who also . . ."

"Yes, but they were eighteen years old," I said, for I'd heard that story before. I was filled with sudden panic. How could I get rid of the papers? In a ditch? Impossible. They would flutter up in the wind like sea gulls for anyone to see. Someone might follow them like a trail, straight to me.

"Dangerous documents . . ." Eddie said beside me. "He should have destroyed them."

That was it! Destroy them!

"It'd be nice to light a little bonfire," I said as casually as possible. "It's the right sort of weather for it."

"Yes," said Eddie. "My mother's cut the toes off my shoes because they're too small. So I've got sandals now. A bonfire? It's forbidden."

"*Everything's* forbidden," I said. Eddie knew this only too well. If his mother didn't stop him from doing something, then his brother would.

"Just be glad you're not a Jew," he said. "They're not allowed to do anything. They can't even go to the swimming pool. They can't go out between eight o'clock and six. They can't sit on their balconies. They can't go to the park. They can't ride their bikes. Can't go on streetcars. Can't go to the movies. And then the star, the yellow star . . . I'd like to organize a gang to fight it, a . . ."

"Oh, come on, let's ride."

"It's all very well for you to talk. These tires feel really flat. Hey, what's that?"

There was a strange, ominous wailing noise. It resounded over the whole city. People started to run toward air-raid shelters.

"Air-raid warning," Eddie announced.

"That's all we need," I muttered. "Let's ride on, Eddie."

But Eddie's mother had impressed upon him that he should always go to the nearest shelter whenever there was a warning, even though lots of people just stayed where they were because usually nothing ever happened. He jumped off his bike and I had to follow him.

And then I saw the half-open ashcan. I pulled off the lid and spat the chewed paper inside. And now the newspapers. . . .

A shrill voice sounded in my ear. "You boys! D'you want to get a bullet in the head or something? And stay away from my ashcan. You won't find anything to eat there!"

Laughing loudly, a woman dragged me by the collar into her house. She was the sort of old woman that you don't argue with. Before we knew where we were, we were all sitting in her cellar. Airplanes screamed past above us.

"So far, so good," she said, more to herself than to us. "Usually nothing happens, but it's better to be safe than sorry. There's—"

A burst of machine-gun fire spluttered down very near us. Through the bars of the cellar window I saw elm leaves drifting over the street. But nothing else happened. Luckily our bicycles were standing in an alley.

"That was close," the woman said. "How old are you two, anyway?"

"I'm in my twelfth year," I said with dignity.

The woman looked me up and down. But she didn't say anything. There was a tray of potatoes near Eddie, and a sack of peat next to me. They were probably all she had. Now she sat grumbling to herself, calling the Germans names, blaming them for everything.

"If only Arie were here," she said. "He's my husband, you know. But he had to go and work in Germany."

At last we were able to go. I didn't have the heart to put my newspapers in the old woman's ashcan. I realized uneasily just how many of them were left.

"How far have you got with your chewing gum?" Eddie asked, examining his wheat kernels closely.

"Oh, blast the chewing gum," I snapped.

And I swung my leg over the rear wheel of my bike.

8
The Paper-Eating Pigs

I had never been on Eddie's farm before. Here in the country I began to feel less afraid, less tense. One could see the horizon, and it seemed as though anything were possible in that distant blue mist.

The farmhouse lay on a rise and was surrounded by trees. I could hear dogs barking in the distance. A small door opened in one of the outbuildings and then, almost immediately, closed again. A figure in blue overalls came out of the house. Cackling and crowing rose up on all sides as the man walked toward us. He looked at me searchingly, and then nodded at Eddie. A dog was jumping up around him. There were pigs there, too; I could hear them snorting.

"You're in luck. The wife's made pancakes," the man said, and then he bolted the small door that had opened just before.

We ate in a long low kitchen that was hung

61

with copper pans. A lot of people were sitting around the table. I found it hard to believe that the farmer had so many laborers. Or could they be his children? They certainly didn't resemble each other. We ate pancakes, and the farmer's wife promised me two bottles of milk for my mother. I blushed with pleasure. My mother would be thrilled, for she wasn't expecting anything. The farmer's wife nodded and smiled at me. All the same, I still had a heavy feeling in my stomach. It felt like a piece of lead that grew heavier and heavier every minute.

"Go outside while I fill the bottles," the farmer's wife said. "You look as though you could do with some fresh air."

I wandered out into the yard. The pigs were there, grunting and wallowing in the mud. They were eating all kinds of rubbish—one of them was even gnawing the wooden wall of its sty. And then I had an idea! Paper was made from wood, or so I thought. If pigs ate wood, then surely they would really enjoy paper! I looked carefully around. Everything was quiet. Even the pond hardly rippled. From it came the sound of frogs croaking.

Quickly I pulled a newspaper from my pocket and held it under the pink snout of an enormous pig. He looked at it with his stupid little eyes for a while, and then he pushed it out of my hand. I began to perspire. The paper lay on the ground. I could read it quite easily.

"Please, oh, please. . . ." I whispered. The pig opened his mouth and ate the paper noisily. Smacking his lips loudly, he followed it with two more.

"He ate it up, he ate it up," I said softly. How

did that rhyme go again? "Fire will burn you, pig will bite you . . ." No, that was wrong. Now another newspaper . . . I was doing very well.

What was that noise? I started in fright. No. No one there. Everything was quiet, the farmyard and the pond. I'll give him just one more helping, I thought. And then I knew for certain that someone was watching me.

I looked at the barn. The window in the loft was open! I stared at it transfixed. Two dark eyes stared at me from beneath jet-black hair. Then they were gone. It had happened so quickly that at first I wasn't sure whether I was dreaming or not. I ran to the barn, pushed open the door and walked down a passage filled with hay until I came to another little door. I had rushed in so quickly that it swung open by itself. Behind the door was a room. A room with a bed, a table, and some books—in the middle of the hay barn! No one could see from the outside that there was a room there. It was empty and nothing moved. It was this that made it all so creepy. I ran back. Suppose someone had seen me . . . suppose the farmer was hiding Jews there, or British. . . . I had to pretend that I hadn't seen it. I ran outside. Sighing, I brushed the hay from my clothes.

And then I saw the farmer behind me. He said, "How old are you?"

"Er . . . I'm . . . I'm in my twelfth year," I stammered. Now he would threaten me, tell me that I was old enough to . . .

"Well, then, don't give my pigs any more old newspapers," the farmer said. "I've got enough of them myself."

He looked at me searchingly. I went as red as fire. I walked over to Eddie, who was waiting for me in the yard. It had not been a very glorious retreat.

It was hard going with the bikes over the fields. We didn't say very much to each other, although Eddie rattled on about the farm and how they always treated you like a grown-up. I felt very guilty when I remembered the farmer's warning, but I had to admit that he was right. He must have thought I was out of my mind. Well, that couldn't be helped. My thoughts returned to the papers. I'd got rid of about half of them. But what about the rest?

"Let's light a bonfire, Eddie," I said as we passed a stack of branches lying on the bank of a ditch. I had matches with me and I had learned how to make a fire with two matches when I was in the Boy Scouts. Not that I couldn't have worked it out for myself, of course.

"It's forbidden," Eddie began yet again.

"Yes. It's forbidden," I said angrily. "And it's forbidden to be a Boy Scout, and standing in the street with more than two people is a conspiracy against the Third Reich. I know all about that. *Everything's* forbidden. So it doesn't matter if we light a bonfire or not, we'd be arrested anyway."

Even Eddie had to bow in the face of this logic. And when we had lain the bicycles on the bank and started a crackling fire with my matches and the thin branches, he started to enjoy himself.

"Oh look, I've got some old newspapers, too," I said, pretending to find them by accident in my saddlebag.

But Eddie didn't hear me. He had scrambled onto the stone wall to make sure that the coast was clear. With relief I threw a bundle of papers on the flames. I could get rid of them all at last. No one would be any the wiser. The ashes would be scattered by the wind. But why was I reminded now of urns and prisoners? I shuddered as I watched the flames consume the printed words. I had forgotten all the effort that had gone into producing these newspapers. How they were passed around. Exchanged. Catalogued. I mustn't think about that. And Sebastian . . . *don't think about it.* These newspapers threatened the life of my brother now. Burned scraps of paper whirled up into the air.

"Psst! Hey, Dirk, someone from the Home Guard is coming this way! Quick, give me your bottles."

Eddie tumbled down the bank. Nervously he tugged at his saddlebag and took out a bottle of milk.

"The swine," I heard him mutter. "He takes them away. He always does. I've heard about it from the others. . . . Let's hope this works. I'm catching sticklebacks, d'you hear, Dirk? Sticklebacks . . ."

I watched bewildered as he emptied the bottle of milk onto the bank. He rubbed his face vigorously with his sleeve. When the shadow of a man loomed up behind us, Eddie was holding up to the light a bottle filled with ditch water. He looked at it attentively. Two sticklebacks were swimming in it, and a worm.

"Now then, who's given you permission to light a fire here?"

I was stunned when I saw who it was—Gerard's brother. The same pale cheeks, the same small blue eyes, the same round head with stubbly fair hair. He was wearing a long leather jacket. There was a band around his arm. He kicked our bicycles with his boot.

Before he could say any more, Eddie blurted out, "Yes, look, we wanted . . . we thought . . . we're studying nature . . . we're catching fish, look . . . it was so cold for this time of year, and so . . . a fire, only a little one . . ."

Drongers looked disappointed. He was standing next to me on the scorched grass.

"Hmmn," he said. "I may let you go this time, but it'd be better if you applied to do proper work. We need sturdy young men . . . and you spend your time messing around in ditches and lighting illegal fires! Stamp that fire out, you layabouts!" He was shouting now. He kicked out at our bicycles. There was the sound of breaking glass. Milk started to drip slowly onto the grass.

His face took on a mean, sly expression. "I suppose those bottles are full of sticklebacks, too?" he said viciously. "Bah! You're nothing but dirty liars! Just what I thought. Concealing extra food from the people, hey? Undermining the strength of the nation! Taking more than your fair share in secret, instead of working on the production line. Collecting milk, hey, to sell on the black market. Yes, I know, cooperating with the whole gang of capitalist plutocrats. It would be a good thing if your fathers applied for work on the Eastern Front! Understand? Good for nothings! Bolshevists! Don't you know I could arrest you for this sort of sabotage? What exactly *are* you doing here? Answer me."

"We've got a day's holiday. I mean, our teacher is . . ." Eddie mumbled. He was almost in tears.

"Aah! That's right! The conceited teacher. So, they've got him at last. A Bolshevist who thought he could help the Anglo-American liberators. Liberators? *Enemies!*"

He was getting very excited. We stared ahead of us, trying to look as stupid as possible. Drongers pulled my bicycle upright, gave it another good kick, and said, "Now, I'll tell you something, my boys. I'm going to let you go this time. I'm not really as bad as all that. I want to do the best for our people, just as our German protectors do. Especially the young people. You could become useful members of our youth group. That farmer, I'll get him one day. But you . . ."

Suddenly he took hold of us by our collars and dragged us over to a big tree. Terrified, we saw a piece of paper hanging there.

"Read it out loud!" Drongers ordered. And Eddie read:

"Death penalty. The following were sentenced to death by order of the Commissioner-General of Security in Amsterdam for contravening military regulations: Jan Jansen, farmer; Piet Mareels, farmer's son; Herman de Boer, agricultural laborer. The sentence was carried out in Amsterdam the third of September 1943."

Eddie was hoarse by the time he had finished. My teeth were chattering.

"Why?" I said.

"Because they found it necessary to persuade neighboring farmers to refuse to supply food to the Germans," said Drongers, irritatingly calm. *"That's* why. And now, off with you!" he roared in a dreadful voice.

We rode away, wobbling on our bikes. Behind us, the remains of our miserable little fire were still crackling. We didn't know what to do now.

"What are plutocrats?" I asked, just for something to say. But Eddie didn't know. "And Bolshevists?" I persisted.

"They're people in Russia. Dirk, look, I . . ." And Eddie began to cry.

"Oh, stop that whining!" I shouted. I was frightened. "What's wrong? Surely everything's going to be all right."

"Yes, of course, Dirk. But I've got to go back.

Warn the farmer. He . . . he's got people in hiding there, Dirk. You didn't know it, but . . ."

I nodded. "Perhaps it'll never happen." I had heard my father say that so often. But usually it *did* happen. And I knew this perfectly well.

"You saw it yourself . . . that notice . . . the executions. . . ."

"That notice has been up there for ages!"

"Yes, but even so. They're capable of anything—and for nothing. . . . I've got to get back. Now."

What had happened to the quiet Eddie that I knew? It was he who took the lead now.

"You take the bottles," he said curtly. "There are still two left. We'll share them. Then Drongers can't say anything if I meet him again. I'll tell him I've left something behind . . ."

"Your cap," I said.

Eddie nodded gratefully at me over his shoulder. I watched him until he was just a dot in the distance.

9
Roundup

It was now well into the afternoon. My heart sank lower and lower the nearer I got to the city. I still hadn't disposed of all the newspapers. Anything could have happened at home. A bomb could have fallen. . . . The house could have been searched. . . . my brother arrested. . . . I pedaled on without seeing or hearing anything around me. It had grown colder and I felt frozen, inside and out. The whole journey had been a waste of time. Nothing had changed. Just pancakes in my stomach. And what help was that? I still had a pocketful of newspapers. And there wasn't a fire to be seen now. No ashcan, no stove, no pig to eat them up. I no longer knew what to do. I felt sick whenever I thought about it.

On the outskirts of the city I saw a piece of brown paper fluttering across the street. I got off my bike and picked it up. I made a neat flat parcel with some of the newspapers and put it in my saddlebag. I would leave it somewhere after a while. In the gutter, perhaps.

I was now in the city. I missed Eddie. I suddenly thought I could hear him rattling toward me on his rickety bike. But it wasn't Eddie, it was a strange man who came pedaling up the street. He was swaying to and fro on the wrong side of the street. I glimpsed the small frightened face of a child behind his back.

I got off my bike. There was an ominous feeling of menace in the air and I didn't know the reason. Why was that man riding on the wrong side of the street? And why was he looking so frightened?

Suddenly a patrol van drove into the street. Rows of green uniforms on the two benches. Rows of helmets. Boots. Guns. The van stopped, and the soldiers jumped down and ran up the street. I turned my bike around. From a distance came the sound of shrill whistles. Run for it, I thought. But, like a reflection of the first, another patrol van drove up behind me. And then I heard shooting. The first van drove slowly away. A bicycle was flung to the ground behind me. A shadow ran into an alley and disappeared. A German grabbed the fallen bicycle, swung his leg over it and rattled down a side street. Pale faces appeared at windows. A harsh voice shouted, *"Ausweis!"* and a man was stopped and had to show his identity card. The patrol van was parked around the corner, just like the one that had stopped outside the school. Was that only this morning? It seemed like a week ago!

I stood petrified in the street. It began to drizzle. My toes felt like dead worms in my shoes. My fingers clutched the cold handlebars of my bicycle. Who was it that had run away just then?

Could it have been the teacher? Sebastian, my brother? My teeth chattered. I peered around me. A woman was beating a rug. A sea gull flew overhead. My eyes seemed like a camera.

I had to get away, I thought slowly, but my brain seemed to be frozen too. It's dangerous here. It's . . . I turned around with one foot on the pedal. And I found myself staring into the face of a gigantic German.

I froze. He had blue eyes, and a square, cleft chin. The letters S.S. were on his helmet and his collar, with a death's-head. I lowered my gaze to his boots. I felt that everyone could hear the newspapers rustling in my saddlebag. The German would search me, go through the bag . . . *Kommen Sie* . . . under arrest . . . I closed my eyes.

"Halt!" said the German. It sounded like a pistol shot. *"Fahrrad.* The Jew. Gone!"

I could hardly believe my ears. He wanted to take my bike! I knew that *Fahrrad* meant "bicycle." I grasped the handlebars even tighter.

"No, you can't, it's my father's *Fahrrad,"* I babbled. I didn't know what had come over me. *"Kann nicht!* My father's bicycle!" And I pulled the handlebars back.

The German stared at me for a moment in

amazement. Then he laughed scornfully. "You little terrorist!" he said slowly. He pulled the bike from my hands with one jerk. I kicked his boots. He thumped my shoulder with the butt of his rifle. I fell against a wall. Blood sprang from my nose and I shut my eyes.

When I opened them again I saw the brown-paper parcel falling at my feet. "*Hier!* Here's your precious parcel, but I'll keep the bottles of milk.

D'you still want to fight? Perhaps you're a Jew yourself!" Roaring with laughter, the German soldier rode away on my father's bicycle. But not in the direction that the fugitive had taken.

I don't suppose that it had all lasted even five minutes. Perhaps not even *one* minute.

"Father!" I shouted. "Father! Father!"

My voice rang through the street. But only the echo answered.

10

The Child
with the Star

I stood alone in the street. It was now as empty
as it had been before. If only I were dead, I
thought. My bike . . . I stared at the ground.
The parcel lay there. The parcel that refused to
disappear. I pushed it toward the gutter with the
toe of my shoe. The street looked as if it had
been painted as scenery for a play. That's how
it seemed to me, anyway. I turned around
quickly. "Home," I mumbled. "I want to go
home."

Behind me a child was standing. A small dark-
haired girl was staring at me with a serious expression.

"Your parcel," she said politely. "You nearly
lost it."

I stared at the child and then at the brown
parcel of newspapers. She pushed the hair out
of her eyes with one hand. And then I saw the
star. It was sewn crookedly onto her coat with

big careless stitches. I realized now who she was. It was the same little face that had gazed at me from behind the back of the wildly cycling man; thin, serious, pale. Hadn't I seen that before? On the farm? . . . No.

"Did you—er—jump off the bike?" I stammered.

"I fell off," said the child. "My uncle started to pedal so quickly . . . he came to fetch me at my house.

Uncle? A chill wind whistled down the street,

the papers rustled. The child and I were the only living creatures on the street. I must have been mad to stay there.

"What's your name?" I said flatly. My shoulder began to ache where the rifle had hit me.

"Hadassa. Atie, I mean." My knee was bleeding, a thin trickle. "There was a roundup. They told me to keep as quiet as a mouse. I sat in the closet for three hours. They stamped through the house. They dragged my brother down the stairs. I saw him between two soldiers through a gap in the closet. My uncle came to fetch me when everything was quiet. He said that he was going to take me to an auntie. But then they came here, too. And I fell off the bike. . . . And then I saw you."

Oh, God. Didn't I have enough on my mind? I had to get rid of this little girl. But the Germans might come back. Perhaps just one soldier on patrol. And then Atie would have hidden in that closet for nothing. I was suddenly seized by a fit of anger. Why me? I fumed. I don't mind helping. It's good to help. In books and things. But I haven't got the time, don't you see? But who was I really talking to? I believed then that two separate people lived inside me. One of them understood everything and nodded his head. The other was crying softly, with his eyes closed.

"Where's your father?" I said sulkily, with my eyes to the ground. I didn't want anyone to see me sniveling in the street. I beckoned the child to walk with me.

"He's gone away," she said. "He had a summons. He had to go to the Dutch Theater one night. They make you go up onto the stage. And then they call out your name. Then you go on a train, the others say. They come for us all the time."

"And your mother?" I asked huskily.

"Gone away too. She went out. Then she wasn't allowed to come back home. I saw them all on the truck, through the gap. My grandfather only had a jar of milk. They pushed him up with their guns."

There was something strange about this little girl. She talked as if . . . yes, as if she were a grown-up. But she couldn't have been more than six years old at the most.

I wanted to ask, "Where do you live?" but then I saw clearly in my mind's eye a sign with the black letters "Jews' Section," the ghetto where the Jews had to stay, guarded behind barbed wire. I started to perspire. Why didn't the liberators come? Why didn't a miracle happen? I couldn't do everything by myself.

"You must go away. And quickly too," I said

in panic. "Look, here comes the streetcar. I've got some money."

"I'm not allowed in streetcars, am I?" the little girl said patiently. She pointed to her star.

I was a fool not to have remembered. "Er—can you ride a bike?"

"A bit. I had a bike once. But they were all taken away. *Your* bike's been confiscated, hasn't it?" She looked at me sympathetically.

"My father's bike, you mean," I grumbled.

I realized now as I never had before just how terrible it must be to be a Jew. They had to be registered. They had to wear a star. They weren't allowed to do anything anymore. They couldn't ride bicycles, or go to the store. Their silver, lead, and copper had been taken away first of all. They had to be indoors earlier than we did. And then they sat in their houses and waited. Every ring at the door could be for them, every knock the signal for their death. One could see now what an evil man Hitler was. How could he do all this? First there was me, scared to death at being discovered with my secret newspapers. And now this little girl. How old was she exactly? He should come here himself, to the center of Amsterdam. Then he would see that we were all just ordinary people, ordinary children with ordinary fathers and ordinary mothers. He didn't need us.

"I've got to help her," I said fiercely to one half of myself. "Yes, but how?" the other half asked ironically.

We were now standing outside an old wooden coffeehouse. Sebastian had bought me a cup of ersatz coffee there once. Suddenly I knew that my legs couldn't carry me a moment longer.

"Come along," I said. And I dragged Atie into the little building. We sat down. We drank our coffee in small gulps. But no sooner had I lifted my eyes over the edge of my cup than I started to choke. I always read anything I saw and I had deciphered the inscription on the window. It read, in mirror writing: "No Jews Allowed."

I put down my cup with a thump. "Hadassa . . ." I said earnestly.

The child looked at me inquiringly, a look that cut straight through me. I realized suddenly that nothing was more important than bringing this child to safety. I could see the trains full of people. Not just people, but fathers, mothers, children.

"Listen, Hadassa," I went on, "everything will be all right. Just do exactly what I tell you."

I stared at the star. Hadassa followed my gaze. "I sewed it on myself," she said proudly.

I peered around. There was no one near us. I pulled the star from her coat with one tug and put it in my pocket. And then, all at once, I had such a pain in my stomach that I just had to go to the toilet.

"Back in a minute!" I called.

There wasn't any toilet paper in the bathroom, only a piece of torn newspaper. I unfolded it.

. . . be carried out and anyone who obstructs this necessary course of action, or attempts to prevent the execution thereof, must, irrespective of his nationality, expect to suffer the same fate as that of the Jews.

I noticed that it was today's newspaper. I crumpled it up quickly, as if by doing so I could rub out what I'd read.

Then I felt my pockets. I still had some newspapers left. I looked up. My gaze fell on the chain and that gave me an idea. Once there had been a raid on my brother's school. The bigger boys had warned the others: "Has anyone got any forbidden stuff on them? Then get rid of it. Down the drain!" Wait a bit. . . .

Furiously I dragged a couple of newspapers from my coat pocket, tore them up, pulled the chain . . . and yes! They disappeared into the depths with a deafening deluge of water. Delighted, I took out a third paper. I pulled again . . . oh, help! Pieces of the paper that had gone before came floating up to the surface. I pulled the chain in panic. . . . I pulled again. . . . This time they stayed down. But I didn't dare try any more.

I stared at the door. Surely the latch had moved! It moved again, slowly but surely. There was someone there! Trembling, I crammed everything back into my pockets. Suppose the newspapers blocked the pipes and flowed out into the street! I shut my eyes. I've got to get out of here, I thought. Hadassa . . . Atie . . .

And then someone rattled the door. A shrill voice called, "Aren't you ever going to come out of there? I've been standing in line all morning for the rations, for those stupid brown beans and a little pot of molasses. Now my bladder's bursting, I tell you! And you lounge around in there as if it belongs to you! *D'you hear me?* You're sitting there smoking on the sly, aren't you? I saw you, with your little cousin. . . ."

Smoking! The thought of the smelly tobacco that my father grew in his garden made me feel sick. I pulled the chain again just to make sure. It sounded like Niagara Falls, but I could still hear the shouting outside. "Now look here, are you going to use up all the water? Come out of there or I'll—"

Whistling nervously, I opened the door. A fat woman with a shopping basket stood there. She gave me a nasty look as she went inside. But she had given me an idea!

Hadassa was sitting like a doll exactly where I had left her. I pulled her by the arm. "You're my little cousin," I whispered. "And don't say anything."

She looked at me. "I'm used to keeping quiet."

She came with me willingly, even when I dragged her hurriedly across the street. I knew what to do now. "Cousin" had reminded me of "aunt," my Aunt Tina. Hadn't she said that she would have taken those Jewish children into her home? And now I had one for her. My aunt would be grateful. I hurried with the little girl over the bridge and along the side of the canal. I rang the bell and then I literally fell into the hall, for my aunt always opened her door without warning. Hadassa fell in over me. It must have been an extraordinary entrance.

"Child," said my aunt in alarm. "Child . . . Dirk? But you look worn out, boy. Tell me, what's happened?"

Watch out, I told myself. Don't cry now. *Don't cry.* She sounded just like my mother. But then they were sisters, after all.

"No, Auntie, nothing. I mean, not to me, Auntie. But Hadassa . . . Atie, that is . . . her uncle took her away on a bicycle. The Germans chased them. Then she fell off the bike. Her father's been taken away, and my bike's been confiscated."

My head started to swim.

My aunt took my face in her hands and gazed at me. She had beautiful eyes. "Hush, now," she said. She drew me to her as if I were a little boy. "Everything's going to be all right. Hello, Atie. Come in, child. You can stay here."

"Always?" the child asked.

"Always," my aunt assured her.

"Then perhaps I can go back to school in September," said the little girl.

I wanted to run away. I had to get home. But Aunt Tina held me back. "Just a minute, Dirk. You've done a very fine thing. Now go home. And stay away from here for the time being."

I was eleven years old, but she treated me as if I were a grown-up.

"Everything's going to be all right," she said again.

And I believed her. I felt suddenly free.

11

The Fight
with Sebastian

But when at last I turned into my own street, all my self-control deserted me. I slumped against a wall and cried, mainly from anger, because everything had gone wrong.

As I staggered up the stairs, my brother Sebastian came out of his room. He started to shout, wild with pent-up fury. "You . . . you've been in my room! What on earth possessed you . . . what have you done with . . . where are . . ."

My father gave him a push and he fell onto the stairs. That's how the German soldier pushed me, I thought. But Sebastian screamed on. "You've got a nerve, you snotty-nosed, irresponsible . . ." He was choking with anger. "He took them, all the papers in my room. . . ."

Then I shouted right into his face, as I had never dared before: "That's right! I had to do it! And I don't care what you think. I'm always too young, aren't I? But you're the one who should have been worried! They could have searched the house. You could have been put in a camp. And Mr. de Lange has been arrested. And little Hadassa . . ."

I didn't know what I was saying anymore. Black specks floated here and there in the passage. From the distance came Sebastian's angry voice. "My documents, my papers, he's stolen them! It's insane, it's too . . ."

"I haven't stolen your horrible papers!" I was screaming now, wild with rage. I no longer saw who was standing there in the passage. I didn't care about anything any more. "Papers! Your rotten papers! D'you think I didn't want to get rid of that rubbish? Beast! Pig! Animal!" I exhausted my stock of abusive language. "Look, here are your papers, here, and here . . ."

I pulled them out of my pockets. I tore open the parcel. The newspapers fluttered along the passage and into the kitchen. I scattered handfuls of torn paper down the stairs. There was a sudden deathly silence. They stood staring at me in horror.

Then Sebastian said nastily, "Hey, have you gone mad?"

The next moment I was fighting my brother as I never had before. All my suppressed rage and bitterness came flooding out. I bashed his head on the kitchen table. He grabbed the tea tray, and when he stood up and came at me, he dragged it with him, and all the cups, glasses, and plates. The smell of ersatz tea filled the kitchen, and the wet tablecloth landed on top of me.

It had only lasted a few seconds. Then my mother came between us. Up till then she had watched everything in silence. Now she took me in her arms as if I were a little boy. And, just as Aunt Tina had done, she said, over and over again, "Dirk, dear, what's happened? My love, everything's going to be all right."

"No!" I shouted, sobbing with misery. I didn't care who saw me crying now. "It's *not* going to be all right. I've betrayed my country, I've betrayed my family. . . the teacher. . . . The secret papers, I gave them to him! That's why I had to get rid of everything. It was so dangerous. They would have come . . . they would have taken everyone away, Sebastian, and Father, and you too, perhaps, Mother. . . . Hadassa's mother . . . I wanted to do something, too, don't you understand? Why am I always too young? You . . . you . . ." I was almost choking with misery.

"Tell me everything, from the beginning," said my mother.

And I did.

12

"I Wanted to Do Something, Too"

"I wanted to do something, too," I finished. "And now I've done nothing at all. That's the worst part."

"Nothing?" my mother asked. She turned my sulky face toward her. "Don't you realize that you've done more than I have?"

I didn't understand what she meant.

"Hadassa," she said softly. "Atie."

"I hadn't thought of that," I said.

My father came back. The whole kitchen smelled of scorched paper. "I stood by when Jews were pushed into trucks," he said. "And I did nothing. I'll always carry that memory with me. I wanted to do what you have done. I'm proud of you. But you must never again do this sort of thing by yourself."

"Oh, no," I said earnestly. I knew that it wasn't a game.

"Anyway, it's turned out well after all," my father said. "And the little girl is safe."

"Yes," said my mother. *"This* time. But, Aart, when is it going to end? We can't put up with all this much longer. So much injustice. So many restrictions. Even the children are frightened now. . . ."

I pulled at her sleeve. "Quiet," I said. From outside came the sound of marching soldiers. They must have been a couple of streets away.

"On the hillside grows a little flower . . ."

"Those voices!" my mother whispered. "Like dogs . . . All that violence, because they're blinded by an evil leader. Those boots . . ."

"Yes," said my father. "But it must come to an end one day. 'Nation shall not lift up sword against nation, neither shall they learn war any more.' It can't go on forever. You must always remember that."

That night my brother Sebastian and my father went to sleep somewhere else, to be on the safe side. They did this quite often. All the papers had been burned now.

"Sleep well," my mother had said. But I couldn't sleep. There was a full moon. Airplanes droned over the roofs through the black night. And droned back. I turned restlessly in my bed. Please drop just one bomb on Hitler's house, I

thought. Please set fire to the police headquarters. Would they execute the teacher? Or
deport him? Would they accept a ransom? Then
perhaps we could . . . I turned over, wide awake.

And then I dreamed terrible dreams. I saw
Sebastian shot dead by the Gestapo. And then,
the next moment, Gerard Drongers was creeping
up treacherously behind the teacher's back. Then
I saw myself. I fell into the fire by the ditch,
I was wearing a helmet with a death's-head on
it. . . .

I was awakened by the sound of a loud voice
downstairs. It was some time before I realized
that it was the milkman. "Now wait until you
hear this . . ." It was reassuring to hear his fa-
miliar voice. I listened.

". . . did I tell you that my brother was arrested by the Germans? For shouting insults at
the soldiers? Well, a German car came to our
place. *Kommen Sie mit uns.* Bring you back right
away. Anyway, they shoved him into the car and
off he went. Then my father said to me, 'Jan,
didn't you fish a German out of the canal?' Well,
I had. And I still had the letter with everything
written down. I was telling your boy about it
just the other day. Anyway, we wrote a lovely
letter to the commander-in-chief. That we'd

pulled one of his soldiers out of the canal and that he'd have drowned if we hadn't. And that we hadn't taken a reward for it, or a bottle of schnapps, or anything. So surely the general wouldn't kill my brother, who was now in prison. . . . And what d'you think? Early this morning . . ."

My mother said something inaudible. By now I was out of bed.

"Early this morning my brother was kicked out of prison! With a lot of others. The teacher was one of them, they say. He jumped on a streetcar first thing but he ended up at the Central Station by mistake. He'd taken the wrong streetcar, you see. Number twenty-four. The conductor looked at him as if he was mad. 'Haven't you got a ticket?' he said. 'No, I've just come out of prison.' So he borrowed some money from a man for the ride back, and now he's . . ."

I didn't wait to hear any more. I pulled on my clothes. I tore down the stairs. Out of the door. To Mr. de Lange's house.

Johanna opened the door. And we were sitting at the table together when he came home. The teacher put a small bundle of clothes on the table, and then sat down with us.

"Well, then," he said. He cleared his throat a couple of times and said again, "Well, then."

And then he began to cry. I thought that I would die of fright and horror. A great big man crying! I wanted to get away. But I couldn't.

Mrs. de Lange put her arms around his shoulders. "Did they beat you?" she asked softly.

He nodded. Then he said hoarsely, "That's not important, Hanna. But you . . . anything could have happened . . . and you, Johanna . . . my children . . ." He meant us, his class.

"Sir," I said in despair. "It was my fault. That newspaper, the paper in your pocket . . ."

I think he noticed me then for the first time. "You're here too, Dirk," he said in surprise. Then he shook his head. He'd realized what I'd said. He looked straight into my anxious face. "No, you stupid boy. You don't think I'd walk around with something like that in my pocket, do you? I . . ." He blew his nose.

Johanna's mother said that she still had a bit of real coffee left. And the teacher began to talk in fits and starts, half to himself and half to us.

"Arrests and interrogation . . . intimidation. . . . It happens all the time, doesn't it? Picking on people here and there. They might let you go for lack of evidence—or not, of course. In the end they shot ten people, on the street, without trial—guilty or not. We didn't realize that these things really happened. Dirk, my boy, I'm glad to see you. But go home now. Tell your father that everything's all right. He'll know what I mean. Don't worry any more than you need to. It isn't playing games . . ."

He raised his head with a jerk. He had dark circles under his eyes. From outside came the sound of stamping boots, and a song. The song I knew so well.

"On the hillside grows a little flower (pom pom pom) And it's called (pom pom pom) E-ri-ca!"

I shuddered at the sound.

"They're only going to the swimming pool," Johanna said calmly.

We all began to laugh hysterically. After a while I didn't know whether I was laughing or crying.

And that is everything that happened on those days in 1943, when I was eleven years old.